USBORNE FIRST READING
Level Three

USBORNE FIRST READING

The **Dinosaur**
Who Lost His **ROAR**

Russell Punter
Illustrated by Andy Elkerton

Illustrated by
Mike Gordon

USBORNE FIRST READING

**Chicken
Licken**

retold by
Russell Punter
Illustrated by Ann Kronheimer

USBORNE FIRST READING

The
**Three Little
Pigs**

retold by
Susanna Davidson
Illustrated by Georgien Overwater

The Musicians of Bremen

Based on a story by
The Brothers Grimm

Retold by Susanna Davidson

Illustrated by
Mike and Carl Gordon

Reading Consultant: Alison Kelly
Roehampton University

Once upon a time, there was a very mean man.

He was mean
to his donkey.

CORN

3

He was mean to his dog.

He was mean to his cat.

He was very mean to
his rooster.

"I'll get him tomorrow.
We'll put him in the pot
and eat him for lunch."

That evening, the
rooster crowed as hard
as he could.

"What are you doing?"
asked the dog.

8

"I'm crowing for the last time," said the rooster.

Tomorrow I'll be rooster stew.

"The master is putting
me in his cooking pot."

"Oh no he's not!" said
the donkey. "He must
be stopped."

11

The four friends set off
at once.

They walked until
they came to a deep,
dark forest.

14

"Wait!" called the
rooster. "I see a light."

It's coming from
a cottage.

The four friends
crept closer.

16

The donkey looked
inside.

"What do you see?"
asked the dog.

"Food and drink," said the donkey.

"And a gang of robbers."

"If only we could get inside," said the dog.

"We can!"
said the donkey.
"Here's my plan..."
19

The donkey
stood near the
window.

The dog leaped on
the donkey's back.

20

The cat climbed on
top of the dog.

And the
rooster flew
on top of
the cat.

"One, two, three..."
said the donkey.

The donkey, the dog,
the cat and the rooster
BURST into the room.

"Help!" cried the robbers. "Run for your lives."

They ate...

and ate...

and ate...

and ate.

30

And then
they slept.

31

The robbers saw the
lights go out.

"We shouldn't have
run away," said the
robber chief.

"Go and see what's
happening in the house."

33

The smallest robber
crept into the kitchen.

He saw the shining eyes
of the cat.

"Burning coals!"
he thought.

"I'll use them to light
my candle."

He put his candle in the
cat's eyes and...

...she leaped at his face.

The robber ran to the
door...

...where the dog bit
his leg.

The robber ran across
the yard...

...and into the donkey.

"Cock-a-doodle-doo!"
screeched the rooster,
flying across the roof.

"Aaaargh!" screamed the robber, running away as fast as he could.

"There's a horrible witch in the house," he panted.

"She spat at me and scratched me."

"There was a man with a knife by the door."

He stabbed me in the leg.

"In the yard there's a
big, black monster."

The robbers never went
back to the house
again.

As for the
four friends...

...they never did go to Bremen. And they never did become musicians.

They liked the house so much they stayed there for the rest of their lives.

The Musicians of Bremen was first
written down by two brothers,
Jacob and Wilhelm Grimm. They
lived in Germany around two
hundred years ago. Together they
collected hundreds of stories.

Series editor: Lesley Sims
Cover design by Non Figg

First published in 2007 by Usborne Publishing Ltd., Usborne House,
83-85 Saffron Hill, London EC1N 8RT, England. www.usborne.com
Copyright © 2007 Usborne Publishing Ltd.

USBORNE FIRST READING
Level Four

USBORNE FIRST READING
The Dragon Painter

retold by
Rosie Dickins
Illustrated by John Nez

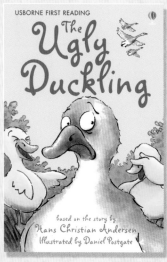

USBORNE FIRST READING
The Ugly Duckling

based on the story by
Hans Christian Andersen
Illustrated by Daniel Postgate

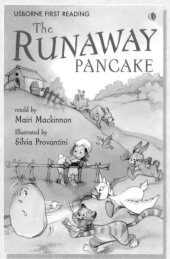

USBORNE FIRST READING
The RUNAWAY PANCAKE

retold by
Mairi Mackinnon
Illustrated by
Silvia Provantini

USBORNE FIRST READING
Little Red Riding Hood

based on the story by The Brothers Grimm
Illustrated by Mike Gordon